A day without a friend is like a
pot without a single drop of honey left inside.
Winnie the Pooh

I dedicate this book to all the children
of the world who are making their
parents proud during this epic time of
Covid 19.

FIRST EDITION

YIPPPPPEEEEE … The world is coming out of Time Out and we don't have to be in Camp Quarantine any more!

Dad said, "Bruno, be careful of the bad germs because we aren't out of the woods yet."

I didn't even know we were in the woods!

"MOM … why do I still have to wash my paws so much? I know … I know … 30 seconds of washing!

This is the way I wash my hands, wash my hands, wash my hands. This is the way I wash my hands to keep the germs away!

COOL … my paws are all wrinkly now!

Finally Mom and Dad let me invite Cousin Bella to play at our house. I thought we'd play pirates, but she came dressed as a butterfly and has been dancing around our house in her tutu.

Mom took a bunch of pictures of us together, but we just wanted to play, play, play! Out of quarantine!

I made a really cool pirate ship and invited Bella to come aboard!

"ARGHHHHH Matey! I'm Captain Bruno from the BB Pirate Ship. You, land lubber, will have to walk the plank and watch out for crocodiles below."

Bella didn't want to come aboard the BB Pirate Ship and had her own plan.

"Bella, I don't want to play tea party. I want to play pirates."

Bella said, "Lets compromise."

"What's COMPROMISE?"

Bella said, "Bruno, would you care for a spot of tea with your crumpets?"

"HUH? Why are you talking like that and what are crumpets?"

"Bruno, I'm talking with a British accent!"

"If you're talking British, can I talk Pirate? Would that be a COMPROMISE?"

"Arghhh matey, the crumpets are good but mighty difficult to eat with my hook and sword!"

TODAY IS MY 7th BIRTHDAY!

I love my birthday breakfast.

"MOM … next year you might need a longer donut!

There's barely enough room for seven candles!"

I'm so happy we're out of quarantine because I can have a party! And invite three friends. And have cake and ice-cream with honey on top … And play games! This is going to be THE BEST DAY EVER!!!"

All my favorite friends came to my birthday party. Cousin Bella, Buddy Bear (my best friend since forever) and Uni Corn who lives down the street. Mom made me a delicious cake and ice-cream topped with honey and sprinkles.

"MOM ... DAD ... we're ready for games now!

WHAT??? You have a surprise for us?

What is it ... what is it?"

YIPPPPEEEEEE!

We're going TO THE PARK for my birthday party!

UH OH … what are all these new signs at the park?

"DAD … what's social distance mean? Do we need to keep a circle around us called 6 feet? Does that mean six of my feet?"

"Sorry … we forgot … we didn't mean to break
the social distancing rule."

"Uni, you okay? Did you get squished?"

"YES … we're trying to social distance."

"OKAY… we'll use hand sanitizer!"

"MOM … why are you wiping down the entire playground with cleanser?"

I'm just one happy bear … no quarantine … and being with my best friends at the park!

"Buddy, who can swing higher? Let's get DIZZY!"

Mom thinks my fur is really shaggy after four months in quarantine. At the barber shop I had to wear a mask the entire time. Do you know how long it takes to cut ALL MY FUR?

"DAD … I think my summer haircut looks pretty good!"

FINALLY … some of the restaurants are open. Mom
said we can go if we sit far away from other bears.
I chose Mexican because of the spicy tacos but mostly
for my favorite dessert - Sopapillas with lots of honey
drizzled on top.
"OKAY DAD … you can have one LITTLE bite!"

"WHAT???
Camp Grizzly Bear has been canceled this summer? Because of the virus?"

This is the worst news ever - even worse than finding out we were in quarantine! Mom said I could be sad and have a pity party for 15 minutes. I don't think this calls for any kind of a party!

"MOM … do you serve snacks at a PITY PARTY?"

Since I can't go to camp, Dad told me to make a list of all the activities I want to do this summer…things I would do at Camp Grizzly.

"DAD … do you like my Smokey Bear hat? It's just like the one I wear at camp."

Camp Ideas

1. Roast marshmallows & make s'mores

2. Camp outside in a tent

3. Look for wild animals

4. Tell ghost stories by the light of a full moon

5. Go swimming

Buddy and I put up our tent in the deep dark forest. We were really tired after all the hard work. I'm pretty sure we're going to stay up ALL NIGHT and tell ghost stories by the light of the full moon!

"MOM … Can we come inside? It's really hot out here and there's no food in our tent!"

Buddy and I love making s'mores with marshmallows, graham crackers, and chocolate squares. I like mine burnt to a crisp.

"Buddy, my tummy's about to blow up. I ate 4 s'mores and 13 marshmallows… how many did you eat?"

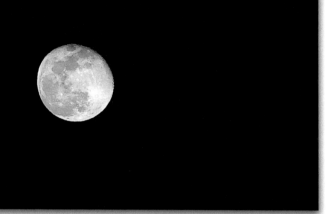

"DAD … LOOK…it's a full moon! Tell us your scariest ghost story EVER!"

Once upon a time there were two best bear friends. They walked single file along the narrow pathway deep in the dark, DARK woods. Tree branches scratched their faces and scary noises made them jump at every turn. Bruno no longer heard his friend Buddy behind him. He turned and reached out his arms to feel for his friend. "Buddy Buddy, where are you? … BUDDY?" NOTHING! Fear crept along his spine from his toes to the top of his head. All of a sudden….

BOO!!!

Dad grabbed Buddy and me and we screamed and jumped to the moon and back. "Tell us another! PLEEEEEASE?"

I wanted to make sure I checked off everything from my summer Camp To Do list. Dad helped me see lots of wild animals and took my picture with my favorite relative.

"Do I look as big and strong as a Giant Grizzly Bear?"

AHHHH… my favorite camp activity - a day at the pool!

"YES … MOM … I've got lots of sunscreen all over my body!"

Yawwwnnnn … time for a little sun bath!

"MOM … DAD … I learned during quarantine that I want to fight germs by being …

Super Bear

Watch out Corona Virus … here I come!"

"Thanks Mom and Dad for everything you do to keep me safe and healthy. I'm the luckiest bear ever. I mean … Super Bear!"

What did you do during the Pandemic of 2020?

Place a picture of your favorite summer activity here!